GIRLHOOD
Journeys

Shannon

A Chinatown Adventure
San Francisco, 1880

by Kathleen V. Kudlinski

illustrated by
Bill Farnsworth

GIRLHOOD JOURNEYS COLLECTION®
SIMON & SCHUSTER BOOKS FOR YOUNG READERS

Grateful acknowledgment is made to Corbis—Bettmann Archive for
the use of the illustrations reproduced on pages 68, 69, and 71.

Simon & Schuster Books for Young Readers
An imprint of Simon & Schuster
Children's Publishing Division
1230 Avenue of the Americas
New York, NY 10020

Simon & Schuster Books for Young Readers
is a trademark of Simon & Schuster.

Designed by Wendy Letven Design
The text of this book is set in Garamond.

Printed and bound in Hong Kong

10 9 8 7 6 5 4 3 2 1

Also available in an Aladdin Paperbacks edition.

Library of Congress Cataloging-in-Publication Data
Kudlinski, Kathleen V.
Shannon : a Chinatown adventure, San Francisco, 1880 / by
Kathleen V. Kudlinski ; illustrated by Bill Farnsworth.
p.   cm. (Girlhood Journeys)
"Girlhood Journeys Collection."
Summary: Newly arrived in Victorian San Francisco from Ireland,
Shannon plans the daring rescue of a young Chinese slave.
ISBN 0-689-81138-1
[1. Emigration and immigration—Fiction. 2. Irish Americans—
Fiction. 3. San Francisco (Calif.)—Fiction.] I. Farnsworth, Bill, ill.
II. Title. III. Series.
PZ7.K9486Sh   1996
[Fic]—dc20   96-2068

C O N T E N T S

CHAPTER 1   The Adventure Begins   5

CHAPTER 2   Chinatown   14

CHAPTER 3   Bric-a-Brac   22

CHAPTER 4   Calling Cards   31

CHAPTER 5   "Worthless Trash"   42

CHAPTER 6   A Leprechaun   50

CHAPTER 7   Home   60

AFTERWORD   Journey to 1880   68

CHAPTER ONE

THE ADVENTURE BEGINS

"This can't be our house, Mamma." Shannon stood in the muddy road. "It's far too grand." A horse whinnied behind her as a moving man pulled a barrel off the wagon.

"Perhaps you're right," Mamma teased. "But those do seem to be our trunks going in. Shall we move in here until the real owners come?"

"Just look at the yard!" Shannon spread her arms wide. "And all the windows, and the porch and the fancy edges on the roof, and . . ." She paused to pull her shawl back up over her red hair.

Papa hugged Shannon. "Easy, lass, it *is* all ours. Leaving you back in Ireland was the hardest thing I've ever done." He reached for Mamma's hand. "But now you're all here, and I've a house and a business grander than any of our dreams.

San Francisco has so much more to offer a doctor than our poor old village ever did."

"Go on inside, Shannon, if you want." Mamma picked up baby Sean. "We'll bring the boys." Papa grabbed little Timothy, but when he reached for Michael, the six-year-old pushed out his lower lip and shook his head. Shannon tried to walk up the path as slowly as the rest of her family did, but her feet wouldn't obey. She found herself racing ahead, up the stairs, across the wide porch, through the door and right into a man carrying a pile of suitcases.

"Whoa, little Colleen, hold your horses!" He laughed and helped her back onto her feet.

"That's none too likely with her." Papa strode through the door, shaking his head. "She's like the fairy folk, moving too quick to think what's right."

Shannon knew she'd been scolded, but she shivered with delight. Fairy folk weren't real, but they were powerful. She knocked on the wooden floorboards for luck and smoothed her apron back into place. "My name's not Colleen," she told the moving man. She caught her mother's eye and quickly added, "But pardon me, sir, and thank you, too."

"We call any Irish lass a 'Colleen,'" he said. "There's a passel of them in this fair city—and lots of other newcomers besides." He tipped his hat and went outside for another load.

"All the furniture we brought on the boat could fit into the corner of one room." Mamma looked around at the empty parlor and sighed. "We'll need more to fill a manor house like this."

"And servants to help us," Papa said.

"Shannon and I can manage just fine," Mamma said firmly.

Shannon looked at her father. "That is the way people live here in 1880," he said with a shrug. "We O'Briens came to America so we could be free—free to be Catholics, free to own our own land and a beautiful home, and free to vote to be sure we stay free!"

Shannon grabbed the silver shamrock at her neck and squeezed it hard. She had always loved hearing her papa talk like that. He'd talked about freedom on the dock back in Ireland, when he'd kissed her good-bye and given her the silver symbol of St. Patrick. And now they were all here, together again at last! She put her arms out and spun in a circle of joy.

Suddenly she stopped. "Where's Michael?" she asked. Mamma gasped, and Shannon raced down the hall, looking for her brother. While her parents called for him out in the yard, she ran up the long staircase. "Michael!" she yelled. "No fair hiding!"

Shannon looked into room after room, each large and empty. No curtains, no rugs, no paintings, no Michael. She checked behind piles of trunks and barrels, then ran to the front windows and looked down. Her parents stood in the street, calling. A beautiful lady stepped out of a nearby house and a man pulled his buggy to a halt. Mamma was wiping her eyes. Shannon's cheeks flushed with anger. It wasn't fair for Michael to spoil this day, she thought. *Why* did she have to have brothers?

"You just wait 'til I find you, Michael O'Brien!" she shouted as she stamped up the stairs to the third floor. Down the hall was an open door. Beyond it was Michael, and beyond him were two big windows. "There you are!" she cried, then gasped. "How beautiful!" Below him and beyond stretched the hills of San Francisco, the

bay full of tall-masted ships, hundreds of buildings crowding toward the water, and a great curve of blue sky above.

As she walked closer to look out the window, Michael threw his arms around her skirts and broke into tears. "What ails you?" she asked.

"I want to go home!" he wailed.

"Go on with you," she scolded. "*This* is home." Michael cried harder. Shannon raised the window and called, "Papa, I've found Michael— and I've found the room I want!" Mamma waved and blew a kiss up to her.

"Look, now," Shannon turned her brother toward the window. "You see those hills? They're like the green hills of home, only steeper. The waves are the same, and the fog rolls in thick here, too." They watched as mist swirled around the ships' masts. "Even the seabirds cry and keen like they do at home." Michael sniffled. "There, now." She pulled a handkerchief out of her pocket to wipe his tears. "San Francisco isn't so strange, is it really now? There's a lot of our old home about this new one."

She looked down at the little group of people standing near her parents. The women were all bareheaded, and everyone seemed to be dressed for church. "Very well," Shannon said to herself. She pulled off her shawl and apron and tossed them onto a trunk. When she reached her hand out to Michael, he held it tightly until they were outdoors again.

"Howdy," a blond girl said with a smile as Shannon walked out into the street. "My name is Betsy."

"Howdy," Shannon answered back. Whatever 'howdy' meant, it sounded friendly. Mamma was hugging Michael, but she caught Shannon's eye. "Oh—top of the morning to you," she added. "I'm Shannon O'Brien."

"I'm glad to meet you, Shannon, even if it is too early for calling hours. It will be such fun to have a new girl my own age across the street—you are eleven, aren't you?"

"Ten," Shannon said when Betsy finally took a breath.

"Anyway, we could make window screens together, and plant flowers, and I can't wait to introduce you to Rebecca, and . . ."

"Betsy, who is your new friend?" Shannon looked up at a beautiful young woman. Her hair was as yellow as Betsy's. Her dress was yellow, too, and her gloves and parasol matched. Shannon realized she was staring.

"This is Shannon O'Brien. Shannon, this is my sister, Alva Frye." Shannon looked at the ground. Betsy was so lucky to have a sister!

"I'm pleased to meet you, Shannon." Alva grasped Shannon's hand warmly. "You'll have to forgive Betsy. She tends to be a bit forward. Perhaps we'll see you for tea?"

"Yes, ma'am," Shannon said.

"Tomorrow!" Betsy called as Alva pulled her back across the street. "You'll come for tea, tomorrow?" Shannon smiled and waved.

Shannon's thick wool skirts brushed against her legs as she climbed the steps of her new house. She thought about Alva's sunshine-colored dress. *What can I wear to visit these Americans,* she wondered. *I don't have gloves that match. What am I supposed to do at a "tea"? What if I say something too "forward"? It doesn't matter,* she thought, hugging herself. *I have a new friend and a new house, all on the same day!*

"What are calling hours?" Shannon demanded as Mrs. O'Brien closed the door. "What does 'howdy' mean? How do you make a window screen, and why? What could be wrong with being too friendly?" Shannon took a quick breath.

"I told Michael that San Francisco looked like home, Mamma. Maybe it does, but it is much stranger here than I ever guessed."

"It is for me, too, Shannon love." Mamma slowly pulled her heavy shawl off. "Anything this new is a wee bit frightening." She hugged Shannon. "America is going to be an adventure for all of us." ❖

CHAPTER TWO

CHINATOWN

"Would you care to come with me this fine morning?" Dr. O'Brien asked Shannon after breakfast the next day. "I'm headed down to what they're calling the Chinatown of San Francisco."

"Oh yes!" Shannon cried. Anything to get away from the stream of strangers Papa had coming today to talk to Mamma about a job as cook or seamstress or housemaid.

"Me, too!" Michael pleaded. "Take me, too!" Shannon held her breath, but Papa shook his head.

"This is a business trip, sonny. Shannon knows how to behave." Shannon sat taller in her chair.

Dr. O'Brien clucked at the horses as they drove through the city toward the harbor.

Shannon looked at all the people on the crowded wooden sidewalks. "Papa, were there so many new faces when you went to school in Dublintown?" she asked.

"Yes, lass. But everyone was the same color there, and none wore pigtails." Dr. O'Brien pointed to an old man with a long pigtail hanging down his back. "You get used to seeing this, and all the strange ways of America." Shannon stared at the loose trousers of the Chinese man, then at the brilliant red dress on a fancy lady, then at the faded blue cap on a tall man's head. There was so much to see!

"That man's skin is as dark as peat," Shannon said, remembering the fuel they burned on cold nights in her old home. "Is he a slave?"

"He might have been, once," Papa answered, "before the war between the States. Now everyone's free here." The buggy bumped over ruts and through mud puddles in the road. Horses strained to pull carriages and wagons up the steep hills. The buildings were closer together. Hawkers leaned over their carts of fruit or fish or fabric, calling out to the O'Briens as they passed. The fog was full of the smell of the sea and strange dishes, of sewage and the smoke from a thousand chimneys.

A Chinese man passed, pulling another man in

a little cart. Other Chinese people walked past, uphill and down, carrying huge bundles balanced on poles. More one-man carts passed. The whole street seemed filled with Chinese people, and the air with their excited chatter. Finally Papa pulled the horses to a halt.

"Where are we?" Shannon couldn't read the sign over the shop door. "Is that Chinese writing?"

"My guess is it says 'Pets.' Mr. Wong sells live animals here," Papa explained. "I buy a few leeches from him every week or so. The old fashioned way is the best for healing a black and blue mark." Shannon nodded. She didn't like the look of her father's leeches, but she'd seen them help his patients.

"Do I have to watch you pick them out?" she asked as he helped her out of the buggy.

"No. Just keep out of trouble." Shannon looked up before she entered the shop. A Chinese girl stood in a window above the strange sign, staring right down at Shannon. The girl had just raised a hand to wave, when suddenly she was jerked away from the window. There had been something white on her hand, and a look of terrible fear in her eyes. "Shannon!" Papa's voice floated out the open doorway.

"Coming, Papa," she answered, but she stood as long as she dared on the wooden sidewalk, watching to see if the girl came back.

Inside the shop were rows and rows of bird cages. Shannon stopped. "Papa?" she called. Bright blue and white birds fluttered against the bars. Monkeys pulled at the locks on other cages, and big spotted cats slept in cages along the floor. The store smelled of animal dirt. Frantic chirps and squawks and whinings filled the air.

"Papa?" Shannon yelled. She didn't want to be there anymore. Not with the poor caged animals.

"I'm in here, dearie." Papa's voice floated through a door at the back of the shop.

"The birds . . ." Shannon said. "They're not happy."

She looked at the nearest cage. A dozen birds crowded along one narrow perch. Another bird sat, sick and shivering on the cage floor. "Poor wee one," Shannon cooed. It looked like it was going to die. They all were, Shannon thought.

"You should be free," she whispered. They belonged in a forest, not trapped in a stinking cage. It just wasn't right! Without another thought, Shannon flipped open the catch on the cage door.

About a dozen bluebirds rushed from the cage, filling the shop with the flash and color of their feathers and their joyous song—and then they all were gone through the open front door. Shannon reached in and petted the sick bird.

"Sir!" the shopkeeper rushed from the back room. "Come, sir!"

Dr. O'Brien hurried to Shannon's side. "What's wrong?"

"This ungrateful child has set a cage of precious birds free! She is a rapscallion, a varmint, a . . . no account . . ." the man sputtered as he glared from Shannon to the open door and back. He held a jar of leeches out to Dr. O'Brien. "Your daughter?" he asked, looking at Shannon.

"Aye, Mr. Wong. That she is, but I'm not so proud of her at this moment." Shannon tried to look small.

"I'll pay for the birds ye lost, and the leeches as well, and then we'll be on our way." There was too much calm in Papa's voice. Shannon knew that she would hear worse on the way home.

"Some daughters are more trouble than they're worth," Mr. Wong said. "If you want, sir, I'll take this one off your hands for you. Perhaps you'd like another girl who knows her place?"

It had to be a joke, Shannon thought. She looked up at Mr. Wong's face. He wasn't smiling. Papa wasn't, either. He handed the shopkeeper some money, grabbed Shannon's arm, pulled her out of the store, and swung her up into the buggy. He handed her the jar of leeches and slapped the reins on the horses to hurry them away. Shannon looked back to see the girl standing by the window again. Now she was crying.

"Papa, did you see that girl?" she asked.

"What girl?" Papa said. "All I could see was you—you and Mr. Wong. I have to come here for leeches and medicines, daughter. This is my business. What were you thinking of when you opened that cage?" Shannon pulled her elbows close and sat very still. "What did you think those birds would do?" he demanded.

"Go free," she whispered.

"What?"

"They were in a cage, Papa. And they were

getting sick. They were going to die. Everyone in America is supposed to be free."

Papa kept his eyes on the road as they drove up the hill. Shannon looked at the side of his face. "You'll see many strange things here, Shannon love. Sometimes it is hard, but we cannot meddle in other people's ways."

"But caging poor little birds?" Shannon argued. Papa shrugged and kept looking forward. Shannon sighed. *Why did I have to make trouble today?* she scolded herself. *Will Papa ever take me anywhere alone again?*

In a very small voice Shannon asked, "Am I more trouble than I'm worth, like that man said? Would you trade me away?"

"Shannon, you're a handful, but I'd never give you up. You're like a wild rose, sweet and pretty and fragrant, but so many thorns!" Still he looked at the road.

"Papa, I'll be good. I'll never do or say anything without thinking first."

"Whoa, there. Don't promise more than you can deliver! Just try a little harder. All roses have a few thorns."❖

C H A P T E R   T H R E E

BRIC-A-BRAC

"You can't hurry at this," Mrs. O'Brien said. "Unwrap each piece and rinse it well, first in warm sudsy water, then in hot. Dry it with the tea towel. . . ."

"Yes, Mother." Shannon sighed. She sat on the floor in front of a steamer trunk, surrounded by pieces of crumpled newspaper. Two pails full of steaming water stood nearby. She looked around the parlor room. With the flowered carpet down and the fringed sofa and chairs, it didn't look quite so empty. She loved the curtain tassels and the beaded fringe on the tablecloth of the bric-a-brac table. "Remember how everything swayed on the ship, Mamma?"

"Don't you be reminding me of that," Mrs. O'Brien said. She rocked from side to side and pretended to lose her balance. Shannon laughed. "You'll never get me onto another ship as long as I live," Mamma said firmly. She wasn't laughing.

Mamma glanced at the family wall. Shannon looked up. The feather pattern of the wallpaper was almost hidden by all the photographs of grandparents and cousins, friends and neighbors they'd left behind. If they never went on a boat, Shannon thought, she'd never see any of them again.

Mamma sniffled and wiped her eyes, then tucked her handkerchief back into her sleeve. "We've got work to do," she said sharply. "You fill the whatnot shelves and the bric-a-brac table, and it will be nearly teatime."

Shannon looked at the trunk and sighed. There were dozens and dozens of little keepsakes to unpack. It would be nice to see them all again, displayed on the shelves and table, lined up across the mantel and along the window sills, but it was going to take hours!

She carefully washed and rinsed and dried six crystal bells from Waterford and carried them to the shelf. She washed and rinsed and dried seashells and glass figurines and china teacups and carried them to the shelf, too. The trunk still seemed full. Her mind wandered back to Chinatown, to the girl in the window.

"Does this all have to be done today?" she asked. Mamma didn't answer, so Shannon wiped and rinsed and dried a dozen little picture frames. Some held paper silhouettes of the O'Brien children. Others framed more photographs. Still others held flowers and patterns made of red hair and brown, gray hair and white. None of the hair was as black as the Chinese girl's. Shannon had tried to wire the hair she pulled from her own brush into flowers, but it took too much patience. Everything did. Shannon sighed.

"Go and explore the yard, then. Get on with you," Mrs. O'Brien finally said. Shannon leaped to her feet. "And take the boys." Shannon wanted to argue, but anything was better than unpacking.

"Timothy!" she stood at the front door.

"Michael! Mamma says we can play outside for a while." The boys whooped and squealed all the way out onto the front yard. Shannon stopped on the porch. At home, front doors opened onto the street, and hedges hid everyone's backyards, she thought. *This* is *home*, she corrected herself.

Shannon walked along the porch railing, looking up and down the street. Everyone else's porch had furniture on it and planters full of flowers. She pictured the flower boxes she could plant for their own porch. All those porches were like extra rooms for each house. But where were all the neighbors? Buggies and carts went by. Deliverymen and servants with bundles passed. But where were the people who owned the houses?

"Shannon?" Michael yelled. "Bet you can't find us!" Oh no, Shannon thought. She ran off the porch and around toward the backyard. A stone path led through an old rose garden. The sharp, clean scents of herbs filled her skirts as she walked further along the path.

"Michael," she called. "Give me a clue." A giggle floated from a little building beside the stable. Shannon poked her head in through an empty window. Musty smells and dust and giggles rose to meet her. Old flowerpots and towels were thrown in one corner. Rakes and shovels and scythes leaned against the wall. A pile of empty burlap bags lay giggling on the floor.

"I found you!" Shannon cried. She went in through the creaky door and pulled on an old pair of canvas gloves she found on a shelf. They were small enough to fit her hands. When Shannon picked up a trowel, the gloves bent just right to fit the tool's handle. A gardener had lived here, Shannon thought. A girl who loved roses and herbs. She smiled. Betsy had said they would plant flowers together. Did the Chinese girl like flowers? she wondered. Would she ever know? A watering can stood by the door. She stepped out to see how close the well was.

"You forgot us!" Timothy pulled at her skirt. "No fair!"

"Oh, pshaw," Shannon said. "Hide again and I'll go looking for you." And, she thought, for other clues about the people who'd left this beautiful house.

The boys scooted past her and into the carriage house. Shannon found dog leashes and dishes there as well as her brothers. When the boys climbed a tree to hide, she found an old tree fort. Hoops had been left lying behind the stable and two glass marbles were hidden in the grass. "I found you! Now, go hide again," she said over and over, until Mamma called them in for dinner.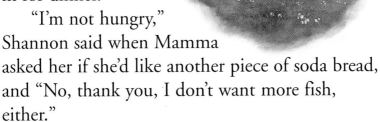

"I'm not hungry," Shannon said when Mamma asked her if she'd like another piece of soda bread, and "No, thank you, I don't want more fish, either."

"What ails the child?" Papa asked.

"She's bursting with hurry to get to the tea party," Mamma explained. Shannon smiled at her. "Why don't you go and change into that pretty frock we bought in New York? I laid it out so the wrinkles won't be so bad."

"Oh, thank you, Mamma," Shannon breathed. She ran up both flights of stairs. All of her furniture was in the room at the top now. She shook out the striped dress. Yellow and blue, her favorite colors. *Mix them*, she thought, *and you get green*. Like the color of home. This *is home*, she told herself again, and stripped off the heavy, woolen dress she had on. Shannon washed at the faucet in the second floor necessary room, then dashed back upstairs to dress.

She pulled on new, lace-edged pantaloons and a chemise. "Unmentionables" her uncle had called them at the store near the docks in New York.

"Unwhisperables" her aunt had called them when they stayed at her apartment between the long trip across the Atlantic and the longer trip around the Cape to San Francisco.

Shannon pulled in her tummy and squeezed her hands around her waist. "No corset yet," her mother had said.

"No corset ever for my daughter," her father had said. "And no bustle." Shannon bundled her apron up and tied its strings around her waist. Then she slid it around backward to see if it would puff out her skirts behind the way Alva's bustle did. Papa would throw a fit, she told herself, and untied it quickly.

Her stockings, her dress, her shoes, and all their tiny buttons seemed to take forever. "Mamma!" she called, running down the stairs with her hair ribbons fluttering. "Would you do my hair?" She handed her mother the brush, whirled around, and stood, panting.

Mamma laughed. "Slow down, dear. You don't need to be in such a hurry. What am I going to do with you? You've missed two buttons on the back of your dress, and just look at your stockings!" Shannon did. The race down the stairs had shaken them down around her ankles.

Mamma waited until she pulled her stockings up, then brushed the tangles out of her hair. "Try to stand still so I can tie these ribbons," she said. Then she coaxed Shannon's wild curls into long fat spirals. "Most girls have to tie their hair up with rags each night to get barley sugar curls like yours." *Rags*, Shannon thought suddenly. *That's what was on the Chinese girl's hand. But why?*

The moment her mother stopped fussing with her hair, Shannon asked, "Am I ready? May I go now?"

Mamma sighed. "You don't want to be too early. Think a spell before you run off. Is there someone who'd like to see you all dandied up?"

"Papa?" Shannon asked. Mamma nodded and Shannon hurried into the front room Papa was making into his office. "It isn't teatime yet, is it?" he asked. Then, "Aren't you the fair young lady?" Shannon turned slowly for a moment so he could admire all sides.

"So quiet, Shannon? Are you worried about something, dearie?" he asked gently.

"Oh, Papa, I want them to like me."

Dr. O'Brien wrapped her in a hug. "They couldn't help loving my wild rose, Shannon. Just think before you speak, and don't let anybody's pet birds go." Shannon looked quickly at her papa's face, but he was smiling.❖

CALLING CARDS

The afternoon had gone on forever, and still Shannon had to wait. "Mamma," she cried. "Isn't it teatime yet?"

"No, dearie. Are you fretting? Sit here by the front window and cut a string or two of paper dolls and I will call you when it's time."

Shannon sat in the wing back chair and looked across the street to the Fryes' house. What if she said something wrong at the Fryes'? What strange ways would she find in the house across the street? She touched her shamrock, shook her head, and whispered, "I'm needing more luck than this."

She began folding a paper strip back and forth, back and forth. With her mother's sharp scissors, she cut out a leprechaun shape dancing on a mushroom. She worked carefully, making sure the mushroom cap's edges and the wee folk's hands overlapped the folds. When she opened the paper, she smiled at the whole fairy ring of dancers and whispered, "Seven leprechauns. That should be luck enough." She folded them up again and tucked them into her pocket.

No one was on the Fryes' porch, so she cut a chain of little girls in hair ribbons, and one of little boys in knickers. Then she tried to cut a chain of elegant girls with their hair heaped high and bustles on their skirts. But it fell apart and she had six cutout dolls. Every one of them looked like Alva.

"Shannon, it is time. I'll watch from the door while you go." Shannon jumped from the chair and gave her mamma a quick hug. She touched the paper leprechauns in her pocket and headed off across the street.

Would Betsy answer her knock and start chattering at once? Or would it be Alva, tall and lovely, and grown-up? When a gray, sour-looking woman opened the door, Shannon couldn't help herself. "Who are you?" Shannon blurted out, then quickly covered her mouth. The woman sniffed and stood aside so Shannon could pass.

"Shannon!" Betsy ran down the stairs.

"Welcome. I'm so glad you're here!"

"I don't think *she* is." Shannon looked back toward the woman still standing stiffly by the door.

"Meeting Eleanor is enough to send anyone into conniption fits," Alva said as she joined them at the door. "She can be as mean as snakes."

"But if she takes a cotton to you," Betsy said, "she's an angel."

"Doesn't anyone here speak plain English?" Shannon asked. Eleanor walked into the hall, her heels tapping angrily against the tiles. She sniffed with disapproval and quickly left. Alva and the girls broke into giggles.

"We haven't made it easy for you, have we?" Alva finally gasped. "Betsy, why don't you take Shannon into the parlor until Rebecca comes?"

"Oh," Shannon breathed. She looked around the formal sitting room. "This is so lovely!" Curios covered every surface, fringe dripped from every edge, and paintings crowded the walls almost to the ceilings. Shannon gazed at sunsets and canyons, mountains and waterfalls.

"Those places were my backyards when I was younger," Betsy said. "Papa is with the railroad and we moved west as the tracks did."

"You lived in the Wild West?" Shannon stared at the paintings.

"Yes, and every morning I said 'Howdy' to the cactus, and the mountains, and the rattlesnakes."

"That sounds awful." Shannon shuddered. "There are no snakes in Ireland."

"No. It wasn't awful. I miss it," Betsy said quietly. "I miss the space and the sky. I miss the smell of sagebrush." *Betsy is homesick*, Shannon realized. She reached for her new friend's hand.

"Here," Alva swept into the room, her skirts swishing. "These are my calling cards. You might like to make some of your own." The girls looked at a little paper card printed with the name "Alva Retta Frye" and a pansy. Alva handed them a china dish. "Shannon, this is the tray where people leave their cards if I am out or I'm not taking callers. You and your mother should have one, too."

The girls looked through the pile of cards in the tray. Each had a name on it with a small picture, such as a flower, a bird, or a lady's hand with a lacy cuff, printed on the front. Some of them had notes written on the back. "The pleasure of a return call is requested," Alva read in a formal voice.

"Do please call for tea tomorrow," Betsy read, in a squeaky old lady's voice.

"We must talk soon. I have news of 'M,' " Shannon read in a spooky voice. They all laughed. "I love mysteries," Shannon said, and thought of the Chinese girl.

"Oh, me, too," Betsy said.

Should I tell her? Shannon wondered.

"We can make calling cards for ourselves and write mysterious notes on them. Shannon, you and I can cut out the cards. Alva, will you do the lettering? Rebecca can do the flowers when she gets here. She is good at painting."

"My card should say 'Shannon Sarah O'Brien,'" Shannon announced in her most ladylike voice. "And could I have a shamrock— and a wild rose—for decoration?"

"Of course." Betsy got paper and scissors out of a drawer. "Mine will say Elizabeth Anne Frye . . ."

"And you'll want a cactus blossom?" Shannon guessed. Betsy answered with a quick nod and a wide smile. "Prickers!" Shannon said suddenly. "Betsy, both of us chose flowers with thorns."

"People had better watch out when the two of you are together," Alva said. "What a bouquet!"

The door knocker sounded and Eleanor's voice floated through the open parlor door, "You'll have to wait here, Miss Rebecca, until I see if they will receive you just now." Alva shook her head. Shannon and Betsy struggled to hold back their giggles.

A slender, brown-haired girl walked into the room, dabbing at her eyes with a lace handkerchief. "Why, Rebecca." Betsy came halfway to her feet. "What's wrong?"

"I was reading *Little Women*—," Rebecca began.

"And you got to the part about Beth." Shannon finished her thought. She could feel her own eyes filling with tears, too. "Isn't it awful?"

"What the Sam Hill are you talking about?" Betsy asked.

"Betsy!" Alva scolded.

"Well, who is Beth and how do you both know her?"

Eleanor entered and set a tray of tea and sandwiches in the middle of the table. "Read *Little Women*, Betsy," she said. "It's a book by Louisa May Alcott. And don't ask any more questions until you do."

"*You* read it?" Alva, Rebecca, and Shannon asked at once.

"One of my favorites." Eleanor actually smiled. "Tea will be ready in half an hour."

By the time tea was served, Shannon had a dozen handmade cards with her name on them. Betsy had made piles of her own and Rebecca was painting dainty violets on the last of hers. While they nibbled at cucumber sandwiches, date bread squares, and ginger cookies, Shannon had told them about the mysterious Chinese girl she'd seen.

"It sounds just like a story from a book," Rebecca said. "What do you think is wrong with her?"

"I don't know. I've never seen anybody look so scared. Or so sad."

"We have to help her!" Betsy declared.

"If I can get Papa to take us back there, will you come?" Shannon asked.

"Oh yes!" Betsy said. "In a trice!"

Just then, Mrs. Frye burst through the door carrying big bags. She stopped, looked at Shannon, and said, "And who might you be?"

"That's Shannon O'Brien, Mamma. She just moved in across the street." Betsy took a bag. "Is this the ribbon? Oh, look!" She pulled handfuls of colored silks out onto the table.

"They'll make beautiful window screens,"

Rebecca said. She spilled dozens of glass beads from another bag onto the tea tray. Shannon looked into the last bag. It held wide black ribbon, colored threads, and a packet of needles.

"Measure out a black sash wide enough to tack across your front window," Betsy told them. "Then pick the color ribbons you want to hang from it as fringe. You have to sew them close together, and stitch beads to the bottom of each ribbon to weight it down. That way they all will hang straight. You'll be able to see out between the ribbons, but nobody on the street will know you are looking at them."

"Oh, look how pretty the light comes through," Rebecca exclaimed as she held a handful of multicolor ribbons up in front of the window. "I think I'll use peach and pale green." Betsy chose red, white, and blue ribbons. Shannon settled on yellow with blue glass beads for weights.

As the afternoon passed, the girls snipped and sewed and rose often to see how their screens would look when finished. "It is a fine and pretty thing," Shannon said, "but what's the harm in being seen through a window?" If there had been a screen over the pet store window, she'd never

have seen the Chinese girl, Shannon thought. She looked at Betsy and Rebecca. Would they really help her? Or was this one of those "American ways" that her Papa had talked about?

"You simply can't have strangers looking at you," Betsy finally said. "Through the window or anywhere else. It isn't safe."

"I've never lived where there were strangers." Shannon reached for another bead. "I knew every person in my village by name and all the peddlers that came 'round."

"There had to be *some* strangers," Rebecca said.

"Sure there were," Shannon agreed. "One would come through every month or so." She paused to thread her needle again. "And of course we'd invite them in for a meal and, if they had need, for a night's stay."

Betsy shook her head. "There's too many people for that in San Francisco. You can't get to know all of them." She held up her window screen. It was almost finished.

"I've got eyes to see that," Shannon said.

"Well, of all those strangers, you never know whom you can trust. Some may be scalawags, or thieves, or swindlers," Rebecca said.

"Or pickpockets, or scoundrels, or murderers," added Betsy.

"I can trust you," Shannon said firmly. "And you can trust me." Suddenly she thought of the Chinese girl in the window. Did *she* have anyone she could count on?

She looked at her window screen, hanging, for now, at the Fryes'. *It's silly to hide from everyone*, she told herself. But she couldn't wait to get home and put up her screen. Its yellow ribbons made the foggy afternoon light look like pure sunshine.❖

"WORTHLESS TRASH"

"Papa, are you going back to Chinatown soon?" Shannon wandered into her father's office. She knew he never saw patients right after breakfast.

Dr. O'Brien looked up from his paperwork. "Shannon, you wouldn't be thinking about going to Mr. Wong's animal shop again, now would you?"

"Yes, Papa." She hadn't been thinking about much else lately.

"Is it about that girl? She's really none of our business."

"Oh no, Papa. It's not about her. Not really." Shannon held her lucky shamrock so tight its edges bit into her fingers. "I just think I should tell Mr. Wong I'm sorry. And Betsy wants to see the shop, too."

"Oh, that's the Frye child? Your new friend seems to be having a good influence on you already." Dr. O'Brien closed his record book. "In fact, I do need to go down that way before noon. The shop carries Chinese cures I don't need, like bears' paws and oriental herbs, but it also has opium and laudanum. I have a patient whose pain is great enough to need narcotics."

"Then we can go with you?" At Papa's nod, Shannon was off to her bedroom. She took one of her calling cards out and sat at her desk. As the breeze ruffled the sunshiny fringe at her window, she flipped her card over and wrote, "Betsy, you <u>must</u> come at 11 today. We have a true mystery to solve in Chinatown."

When Eleanor opened the door, Shannon handed her the card. "May I leave this for Betsy, please?" Eleanor took the card. Before she vanished into the house again, Shannon asked, "Do you think Louisa May Alcott is really Jo, all grown up?"

"It's not my place to think about who a writer puts into her books," Eleanor replied. Then her face softened. "Perhaps," she said, and shut the door.

Shannon skipped back home and finished

unpacking the trunk of whatnots. "Ready, my little rose?" Papa walked into the parlor as she dried the last conch shell.

"You both look fine," Mamma said, after retying Shannon's hair ribbons and smoothing a wild hair on Papa's moustache. Papa sneezed and thanked her, and they went out to get the buggy.

"Shannon?" Betsy called as she crossed the street. "What's the—" Betsy stopped when Shannon put her finger to her lips.

"Your father is going to help the girl?" she whispered, leaning against Shannon in the buggy.

"No. He wouldn't think we should. He doesn't want me to meddle in other people's ways. We're going to have to do it ourselves," Shannon whispered back.

Betsy grinned. "Good. I do love an adventure." Shannon sat quietly, remembering what her mother had said: This American adventure was "a wee bit frightening." This was more than "a wee bit," Shannon thought.

Betsy looked at the street sign as they turned off Taylor Street to Jackson. "I had a cousin who was shanghaied on this very street," she said. "Seth was in a saloon, and they knocked him cold. He woke up on a boat, two days out of San

Francisco, heading for the Orient. We didn't hear from him for nearly a year."

"How can that happen?"

"If it is time to set sail and a captain doesn't have enough crew members," Papa said, "he might kidnap anyone he can get, drunk or drugged, to be cabin boy or oarsman. It's wrong, of course, but it happens."

"Don't they arrest the captain?" Shannon was horrified.

"Once he's out of port, a captain is the law on his own ship." Shannon shivered and leaned against Papa's big shoulder. "Shannon, love, be easy. They don't shanghai girls."

"They do steal girls to sell as servants, sometimes," Betsy said, looking straight into Shannon's eyes.

"We'll have no more talk of that," Papa said, pulling the horse to a stop in front of the store. "Shannon, I'm proud of you, my girl." Shannon squeezed her eyes shut. "You're doing the right thing," he added. "I'll just tie the horse out here while you conduct your business with Mr. Wong."

Betsy jumped out of the buggy. "Shake a leg, pardner." Shannon had to smile.

"You?" The shopkeeper's eyebrows raised as they entered the store. "You!"

Shannon took a deep breath of the shop's foul air. "Sir," she said, "I'm sorry I let the birds go. I meant no harm. They just looked sick. I felt bad for them." She had to take another gulp of air.

"And not for me? You ungrateful thing! You are as bad as Mi Ling here." He pointed a long yellow fingernail at the Chinese girl, crawling on the floor between the cages of wild cats. "You're lazy and careless, wasteful and self-important."

Shannon stepped backward as the man's voice rose. "You can never repay what you cost me!" *Does he mean me?* Shannon wondered wildly. Hadn't her Papa paid him for the birds? The shop girl covered her face with bandaged hands. "You're a disgrace to your—Welcome, kind sir." The shop-keeper's voice suddenly turned sweet as Dr. O'Brien entered. "And what can I show you today?" He smiled broadly.

"I'm after some medicines," Shannon's father said.

"Step into the backroom." Mr. Wong waved toward the far end of the shop, then turned. "And you young ladies feel free to look at all the pretty pets." His voice changed again. "Finish quickly, Mi Ling."

Shannon and Betsy stood looking at each other silently. Papa hadn't heard any of it, Shannon thought. Surely he'd do something. Wouldn't he? Betsy finally broke the silence with a whispered, "Well, gosh durn Almighty."

"Don't swear," the Chinese girl said.

"What?" Both Betsy and Shannon stared down at her.

"Thou shalt not take the name of the Lord, thy God, in vain," Mi Ling quoted from the Ten Commandments.

"You, ah, you speak English?" Shannon asked.

"Yes. It is not you he is angry with." The girl paused to look under the monkey cages. "It is I. A squirrel monkey got free, and I was told to find it before the shop opened today." She stood and stretched her back like an old woman.

"But monkeys bite!" Betsy said.

"Any animal does, if it is cornered and afraid." The girl held up her hands. Both were bandaged and one arm had a long, fresh scar.

"That is your job, to catch loose animals?" Shannon asked.

"And they bite you?" Betsy asked.

"It is not their fault. And Mr. Wong feeds me and gives me clothes."

Shannon looked at Mi Ling's thin face and ragged shirt. "Where are your parents?"

"They died in China, long ago—but hush." Mi Ling looked quickly to the back door.

"Thank you," Dr. O'Brien was saying. "This should serve for a week or so. Mr. Wong said something in Chinese to Mi Ling. She answered quickly, and his voice began to rise again before he turned to Dr. O'Brien. "Do pardon us, kind sir," he said. "This one is worthless trash. I'd trade her for a monkey."

"Come, Shannon," Dr. O'Brien said quickly, "and Betsy. It is time we left." As the buggy pulled from the curb, the shopkeeper's voice floated after them, roaring on and on at Mi Ling in Chinese.

"Would you look at her hands, Papa?" Shannon asked.

"Mr. Wong knows Chinese medicine, daughter. I take care of you the best I know how, and I'm sure that he does the same for that child. His ways are simply different than ours. We're not going to meddle in this new country."

The girls were silent as Dr. O'Brien followed a cable car up Jackson Street toward home. Its bell rang constantly. It rang when people jumped on, and again when they got off. It rang when someone walked in the way or a carriage crossed its path. The O'Briens' buggy horses bobbed their heads and pulled in their harnesses each time they stopped to wait for the cable car to take on or let off passengers. Finally they turned off on Taylor Street, and Papa could hurry the horses along. Mrs. Frye waved at them from the porch, and Shannon suddenly longed for a hug.

"What are we going to do about Mi Ling?" Betsy whispered, stepping out of the buggy in front of her house.

"I don't know," Shannon replied, "but I think it's time to meddle."❖

CHAPTER SIX

A LEPRECHAUN

Shannon scooped soil into the pot and pressed it down around a geranium. "Hand me one of the herbs, please."

"Isn't this supposed to be a flower pot?" Betsy asked.

"I want this planter to make our porch smell as good as it looks pretty," Shannon explained. "Peppermint would be nice, or lemon verbena."

Betsy handed her a catnip plant. "Shannon, sometimes I think you're crazy as a loon." Shannon smiled, then quietly planted the catnip, then another flower, then more herbs to fill the long narrow pot. "Can Alva drive a buggy?" she asked.

"Yes, but she'd rather have Edward squire her around."

"Who is Edward?" Shannon asked. "Don't tell me Alva has a beau!"

"Yes. She has set her cap for a lawyer. He comes courting every few days. It's a stitch to watch them. She sits on the sofa fluttering her eyelashes at him. He sits on the sofa making cow eyes at her. And Mamma sits on the sofa watching the two of them like a hawk."

"Your mamma won't leave them alone?"

"Of course not! My sister is a good girl," Betsy said. "They play chess or checkers or sing together. And Mamma watches. Sometimes they go to lectures and dances. Mamma won't let them go to the theater alone, though, because the lights go out during the play."

"Would she let Edward and Alva drive me to Mr. Wong's shop after supper? If we were back before candle lighting?"

"Not a chance. But maybe we could go to Mr. Wong's alone."

"Just the two of us?" Shannon breathed softly. Alone? "How?"

"On the cable car," Betsy said slowly, "if you're brave enough, that is."

Shannon sat up and pulled her gardening gloves off. "Why not? Nobody would mess with a prickly pair like us." She wished she felt as bold as she sounded.

"Shannon, you do have a plan to help Mi Ling, don't you?" Shannon just looked at Betsy and smiled. She didn't want to tell her new friend she had no ideas at all.

"Well, count me in on the adventure, pardner. I'll meet you here after dinner."

Shannon rubbed her silver shamrock charm all the way into the house, then stopped. *I'll need more luck than a shamrock or a paper fairy ring tonight*, she told herself. *I'm going to need the real McCoy! But where in America can I find a leprechaun?*

She was still thinking about how to get a leprechaun when she found Betsy waiting on the garden path. "Howdy, pardner! Ready to go?"

"Hush!" Shannon said quickly, but it was too late. She could hear Michael's footsteps on the stone path. Betsy, Shannon thought, didn't know anything about living with brothers.

"Me, too!" Michael pulled on her skirt. "I want to come, too."

"No," Shannon said. "You have to stay here."

"I want to go with you!"

"We won't be long," Shannon promised. "And Betsy will play hide-and-seek with you when we get back." She could see the excitement on

Michael's face—and the surprise on Betsy's—even in the dim light. "You might look for good hiding places while we're gone," she suggested to her brother.

"Bye, bye!" Michael said. "Go now so I can look for good hidey places."

Betsy laughed and pulled Shannon down the street. "If we wait at the corner, the cable car will stop for us. You did bring a few pennies, didn't you?" Shannon shook her head. "I'll pay our way, then," Betsy offered, as a cable car slid to a halt on its tracks.

"You girls out alone at this hour?" the conductor asked them as they climbed aboard.

"Yes, sir, and we'll be home and safe before dark," Betsy told him as they took their seats.

"Do you often ride the cable cars alone?" Shannon asked.

"I never have before," Betsy answered over the clanging bell. Shannon closed her eyes and reached for her shamrock. Finally they reached their destination. "Here's our stop." Betsy grabbed Shannon's hand and pulled her off the car. They hurried down the road to Mr. Wong's.

The night watchman wandered down the wooden sidewalk, using his flare to light the gas streetlights. As soon as he passed, a small shape darted over Shannon's feet.

"A rat!" screamed Betsy.

"No, it's not." Shannon was after the creature in a flash. She knew that shape. It wasn't a rat—it was a little man, running faster than wishes. "Catch it!" she cried. "Oh, please, catch it."

Betsy grabbed for it as it scurried under an empty carriage parked by the sidewalk. "Dash it all!" Betsy cried. "I almost had it!"

"I'll get it!" Betsy darted around the back of the carriage, while Shannon ran around the front. The ghostly little man scampered to the carriage roof. Shannon climbed up one side; Betsy scaled the other. "I've got it!" they both cried. They reached the middle of the roof just as the little man swung in through the carriage window.

"Lands' sake! It's on the seat!"

"Grab it," Shannon gasped, climbing down toward the door. The horse started and jerked the carriage, but Shannon hung on.

"I can't get near it." Betsy leaned in the

window. "It's got too many teeth!" Shannon pushed through the door. In one corner of the seat, a tiny monkey cowered, trembling. As it jumped for freedom, Shannon fell across the bench and grabbed it.

"Ow!" she shrieked.

"Hang on!" Betsy said. "I'll put my coat over it." She covered the tiny monkey in Shannon's hands.

A light was lit inside the shop. "Who is there?" the shopkeeper called in English. Then he called out again, this time in Chinese. Shannon and Betsy carried their prize in under the coat.

"You two?" Mr. Wong said. "What do you no-good ruffians want now?"

Shannon thought fast. "Mi Ling," she said. "We've come to trade for Mi Ling. You said you would trade her for a monkey." Betsy pulled the coat off.

"Oh, your poor hands," Betsy said. The monkey and Shannon were bloody, but Shannon wouldn't let go.

"Well?" She stared at Mr. Wong.

Mi Ling slid into the back of the shop. Mr. Wong glanced at the girl. "Did you bring Dr. O'Brien with you?" he asked Shannon, and looked from the backroom to the front door.

"No," Shannon said. "But . . . Betsy's brother-in-law is a lawyer, and he'll take this to court if you don't follow through with the deal you made." Betsy looked at Shannon with her mouth open. "Won't he, Betsy?" Shannon prompted.

Betsy nodded. "The night watchman is coming," she added, "and a constable will be here soon, too."

"The police? You're bringing them here? Now?" Mr. Wong said. "Fine. Take her. Take both of them this minute. The monkey *and* the girl. They're yours—and good riddance."

"Mi Ling!" Shannon cried. "Come quickly!" Mr. Wong darted to the door and looked up and down the street. "Tell the constable that my partners and I have closed down the business," he said, blowing out the kerosene lamp. Two shadowy figures rushed from the backroom and out the door.

Shannon grabbed Mi Ling's hand. "Hurry!" Betsy said from the sidewalk. The girls ran out of the store just before Mr. Wong pulled down the shade and slammed the door shut. He jumped onto the driver's seat of the carriage, cracked a whip, and sped off into the night.

Mi Ling stood on the sidewalk. "There," Shannon told her. "You're free. You can go now."

Shannon let go of the monkey, too. Instead of running, it climbed up her arm and settled on her shoulder.

Mi Ling stood silently, looking at her. "Go on, Mi Ling."

"And just where shall I go?"

Shannon thought for a moment. "Oh," she said, in a small voice. "Oh, dear."

"Well, you sure as shootin' can't stay here waiting for Mr. Wong to change his mind," Betsy pointed out. "Let's run for the cable car."

"Who's she?" the conductor asked, pointing to Mi Ling as the girls climbed into the cable car. Shannon looked at the Chinese girl and her heart sank. Mi Ling was dressed like the guttersnipes who slept on the streets and begged for food. She even smelled like them.

"Pardon me, sir," Mi Ling answered with a ladylike voice. "My name is Mi Ling. I'm a friend of these fine girls, visiting from the Orient. Thank

you for your kindness." Shannon smiled.

"I'll pay her fare," Betsy said. "Now we really must get off the streets."

The conductor rang the bell as the car started again. "You shouldn't be out this late," he scolded them. "You wouldn't believe what can happen to young girls in this town."

As the cable car pulled toward home, Betsy looked across Mi Ling at Shannon and burst out giggling. "What's wrong, now?" Shannon asked.

"Looks like you have a new friend," Betsy said, and reached toward Shannon's shoulder. The monkey shrieked, Shannon jumped, and they all laughed aloud.❖

HOME

"Y ou can stay here tonight, Mi Ling."
Shannon pushed open the big wooden door of her stable. "We'll have to think what to do with you in the morning."

"I can bring you food," said Betsy.

"And I'll get you some proper clothing," Shannon said.

"Thank you, but I'm not a doll to be dressed and petted," Mi Ling said stiffly. "I don't want your help. I'll do perfectly well here tonight, but I will make my own way tomorrow." Shannon gasped, then remembered Mi Ling's own words: "Any animal bites if it is cornered and afraid."

"Well, good-night, Mi Ling," Betsy called softly. The Chinese girl didn't answer.

Shannon shook her head and spread the thick carriage robes on a mound of hay. "You can use

these for a bed if you like, Mi Ling," she offered.
"Over there are the faucets and some soap and
grain bags you could use for towels. Sleep well, Mi
Ling."

"Take care of those hands, Shannon," Mi Ling
called in return. The monkey chittered softly in
Shannon's ear as she left the stable.

What should she do? Shannon wondered. Mi
Ling couldn't make her way back home to Hong
Kong alone anymore than Shannon could get
back to Ireland by herself. Should she tell her
papa? She had never meddled so much in her life.

"Shannon, oh, darling, thank the saints, you're
home!" Mamma called as Shannon's footsteps hit
the porch stairs. "Candle lighting passed with no
sign of you and Michael, then dark fell, and still
no children. We did not know if you'd been
taken—Lands' sake, child! What's sitting on your
shoulder?"

"Never mind that, where have you been?"
Papa demanded. "Do you know what you two
have put us through? Do you have no sense about
you?"

"Mamma, Papa," Shannon looked from one
to the other, "I don't have Michael."

Mrs. O'Brien buried her face in her hands.

"Where is he, then?" Dr. O'Brien thundered. "He's not here. We've searched everywhere for the two of ye."

Shannon thought fast. "When I left, Michael was playing by the carriage house. He wanted to go with me, but I said no. I think he's hiding."

"How do you know that?"

Shannon swallowed hard. "Because I told him to," she said. "I'm sorry. I just didn't think . . ."

Papa shook his head and glared off into the night sky.

"Michael's hiding? In the dark? In a place we don't know?" Mamma sobbed. "At least we thought if he was with you he was safe. Now to think of the wee one all by himself in this dangerous city . . ." Mamma hid her face again.

"I know the yard almost as well as Michael does, Mamma," Shannon said. "I know where he's hidden before." *And,* she thought, *I have a friend to help me look.* "Have you searched the attic?"

"Yes, but we weren't really looking for tiny hiding places." Mamma patted her eyes. "I'll go look once more."

"Mr. Frye went for the police about Betsy,"

Papa said. "He was worried sick, too. What could be so important that you both left without a word to anyone?"

"Let it rest until we find the boy," Mamma called.

Shannon ran back to the stable and told Mi Ling about Michael. "We're lucky there's some moonlight," Mi Ling said, heading out to search. Shannon looked in the shadows behind the well. She peered into the dark garden shed, down the stone path, and behind the bushes.

"Michael!" "Michael!" voices called out in the soft San Francisco air.

"I have found him!" It was Mi Ling's voice.

"Shannon?" Michael's voice sounded sleepy. Shannon rushed to Mi Ling's side and together they led Michael onto the porch and into the gaslight.

"Oh, Michael, my dear, dear wee lad." Mamma swept him up in a hug.

He looked over her shoulder at Shannon and yawned. "I think you have a monkey," he said, then rested his head on Mamma's shoulder and shut his eyes.

"And who is this girl?" Papa asked. He looked closely at Mi Ling. "Isn't she the one from Mr.

Wong's? Shannon," Papa's voice suddenly got deeper. "What have you done?"

"I can explain everything," Shannon said, then stopped. She had no idea how to begin.

"My name is Mi Ling." The Chinese girl's calm voice interrupted. "I am a slave. Your brave daughter thought to buy me this afternoon and says that now I am free. She has been good and kind and—"

"Stop," Papa said. Mamma put Michael down. "Who said you are a slave?"

"A year ago, I was sent on an errand from the English church orphanage in Hong Kong. I was kidnapped and put on a ship, then Mr. Wong bought me to work in his shop. Am I now free?" Shannon reached for Mi Ling's hand. The girl's story was worse than anything she had imagined.

Mamma and Papa looked at each other over Mi Ling's head. "Why didn't you tell me?" Papa asked Shannon.

"You told me not to meddle in other people's ways," she said. "I tried not to, but this was just so wrong, I had to do something."

"Thank the Good Lord you did," Papa said. "But I never meant . . ."

"What's going on here?" A police officer in a

dark blue uniform marched up the steps. "Are
these the children that were lost?"

"Yes, sir," Papa said. "We seem to have found
an extra one, though. Could I speak with you a
moment in the parlor?"

Michael yawned as Mamma led him inside
the house. Shannon and Mi Ling sat side by side
on the steps. "What do you think the police will
do?" Shannon asked.

"Put me into another orphanage, I suppose."
Mi Ling looked at Shannon's face. "It's not so bad,
really," she said, but Shannon could see her new
friend's shoulders slump.

"Maybe," Shannon said, "just maybe . . ."

"Don't bother saying it," Mi Ling said. "I've
learned not to hope."

Well, I haven't, Shannon thought. So she sat,
hoping as hard as she could and rubbing her lucky
shamrock, until Papa and the policeman came
outside again. Shannon held her breath.

"We'll need you to tell your story in court,
young lady. There's laws against slavery in this
country, though not everyone obeys them yet.
We've been trying to break a child slavery ring
here for years, and with your help we could put
Mr. Wong and his friends in jail."

"It would be an honor." Mi Ling's voice was cold and flat and hard. Shannon looked up at Papa. He winked at her.

The policeman continued, "This case won't be going to court for some months, Miss. The O'Briens have offered to give you a home—"

"For as long as you need it, lass," Papa broke in.

"Hooray!" Shannon cried, throwing her arms around Mi Ling. Then she held her breath. After a heartbeat, her new sister hugged her back. ❖

A F T E R W O R D :

JOURNEY TO
1880

S an Francisco streets were full of **immigrants** in 1880. These newcomers arrived from the East by wagon load or on the new cross-country railroad. Others sailed into the great harbor in clipper ships or steamers. All of them

were lonely for the friends they'd left home. All were ready to make new friends and a new life in America.

Shannon and her family and friends are made up, but they face problems that real immigrants faced back then—and still do today.

Where did all the San Francisco immigrants come

Chinese immigrants arriving in San Francisco

from in 1880? From everywhere on earth, but especially from China and Ireland. When the United States government counted in 1879, it found that one-fifth of all the people in San Francisco were Irish and another fifth were Chinese.

Ireland and China were very poor countries in 1880. There were few jobs there and only a few people had any land or money. Most people lived near starvation. San Francisco was a rich town in a wealthy nation. Money flowed into the city from silver and gold mines, huge

Chinese laborers at work on the Northern Pacific Railroad

farms, and the new **transcontinental railroad**. Here, there were jobs for anyone willing to work and money to pay them. Many worked as servants and laborers. There was land for anyone who would farm it. Immigrants longed to give their children the chance to grow up in a country without hunger and a land with freedom.

Sometimes whole families moved together. But often the men, like Dr. O'Brien, came to America first. They found jobs and places to live. Then they saved their money to buy tickets so their wives and children could join them. Most immigrants arrived poor and spent years working hard for low wages. They obeyed the new laws, tried to learn the new customs, and studied hard to become voting citizens in their new land.

Most San Franciscans were good people, but a few were greedy and evil. It was true then; it is true today. There are always some people, from every country, who will break laws to get rich quickly. The police had their hands full in 1880 trying to keep law and order in this city of strangers.

All of those lonely newcomers were trying to make friends. There was no TV or radio, and sending a letter to family and friends in far-off countries took weeks. San Francisco didn't have those "new-fangled" telephones yet, so people couldn't just call each other. They had to go to each other's homes. But imagine if your doorbell rang as often as your telephone! Your family would never have any time to themselves. So visiting was done mostly during afternoon "calling

hours" in the 1880s. And calling cards took the place of answering machines when friends missed each other during calling hours.

To make friends (or do business or run a household) you have to talk to people. The Irish immigrants were lucky: They already spoke English when they came to San Francisco. It was harder for the Chinese, who had to learn a whole new language. Their foreign looks and clothing set them apart, too.

A scene in San Francisco's Chinatown

All the immigrants tended to move into neighborhoods where people from the "old country" already lived. The grown-ups felt more at home around people who spoke, and looked, and behaved in ways they were used to. Their children learned new ways much more quickly. It was true then; it is true today. It is kids like you (and like Shannon, Betsy, and Mi Ling) who build bridges between cultures and into the future. ❖